WHAT GOOD

SHALL I DO

THIS DAY?

BEN FRANKLIN'S

# POOR
# RICHARD'S

ALMANACK FOR KIDS

## New Hope Press

NEW HOPE, PA

Many a home library in colonial America had but two books: the *Bible* and Ben Franklin's *Poor Richard's Almanack.*

The *Almanack* had poems, recipes and weather predictions, and was more than a calendar. Like the *Bible*, it was full of proverbs about virtue. But Ben's book had one advantage the Lord's book did not: humor. (It was rumored that Ben was not asked to write the Declaration of Independence out of fear he would put a joke in it.) *Poor Richard's* was an astounding success, selling 250,000 copies during Ben's lifetime.

In his late twenties, the lightning-quick Ben was busy testing a scientific notion that virtue was the key to happiness and success in life. The best time to begin learning about virtue, Ben said, was in childhood, before poor behavior could become a habit. It was a bit late for that, but the talented young inventor wished to reinvent himself and dreamed up a detailed plan that amounted to a moral makeover. Ben now began and ended each day asking God what good he might do.

The *Almanack*, published yearly from 1733 to 1758, was full of short, funny sayings that focused on some of Ben's favorite virtues. Over 250 years later, they still serve as one of America's favorite sources of folk wisdom. Ben didn't invent them all. He tinkered with ideas from his study of "the wisdom of many ages and nations."

*Poor Richard's* proclaimed that virtue was its own reward, but in Ben's case it brought plenty of earthly benefits, too. With the success of his

*Almanack*, he became the first great publisher in America. Ben was wealthy by the age of forty, and retired to become a scientist and statesman. This was the best frontier for virtue, thought Ben, who believed we please God by service to others.

If we look at this cheerful friend of mankind, with his scientific contributions, his diplomatic triumphs, his role in developing the first libraries and schools, police departments and paved streets, we see that Ben's virtue plan fueled two of his most powerful beliefs: first, in the goodness of the Creator, and next, in the endless potential of the human mind.

We see, too, that being part of good causes can create a good life, that through his experiments with virtue, Ben came to discover joy.

## SELF-CONTROL
EAT NOT TO DULLNESS. DRINK NOT TO ELEVATION.

## SILENCE
SPEAK ONLY WHAT MAY BENEFIT
OTHERS OR YOURSELF.

## ORDER
LET ALL YOUR THINGS HAVE THEIR PLACES.

## RESOLUTION
RESOLVE TO DO WHAT YOU OUGHT.
DO WITHOUT FAIL WHAT YOU RESOLVE.

## CONSERVATION
MAKE NO EXPENSE BUT TO DO GOOD TO
OTHERS OR YOURSELF. WASTE NOTHING.

## INDUSTRY
LOSE NO TIME. BE ALWAYS EMPLOYED
IN SOMETHING USEFUL.

## SINCERITY
USE NO HURTFUL DECEIT.
THINK INNOCENTLY AND JUSTLY.

## JUSTICE
WRONG NONE BY INJURIES OR OMITTING
THE BENEFITS THAT ARE YOUR DUTY.

## MODERATION
AVOID EXTREMES. DO NOT RESENT
INJURIES SO MUCH AS YOU
THINK THEY DESERVE.

## CLEANLINESS
TOLERATE NO UNCLEANNESS IN BODY,
CLOTHES OR HABITATION.

## TRANQUILITY
BE NOT DISTURBED AT TRIFLES, OR AT
ACCIDENTS COMMON OR UNAVOIDABLE.

## HUMILITY
IMITATE JESUS AND SOCRATES.

Eat to live,

and not live

to eat.

A GOOD CONSCIENCE

IS A CONTINUAL

CHRISTMAS.

THE WORST WHEEL

OF THE CART MAKES

THE MOST NOISE.

A GOOD EXAMPLE

IS THE BEST

SERMON.

O RDER

IS INWARD

LIBERTY.

ORDER ALLOWS MORE

TIME FOR ATTENDING TO

PROJECTS AND STUDIES.

How few there are who
have courage enough to own
their faults, or resolution
enough to mend them.

Resolve each

MORNING TO MAKE

THE DAY A HAPPY ONE.

When the well's dry, we know the worth of water.

WHO IS RICH?

HE THAT REJOICES

IN HIS PORTION.

He that waits

upon fortune, is never

sure of a dinner.

THE MOST IMPORTANT

QUESTION IN THE WORLD IS:

WHAT GOOD MAY I DO IN IT?

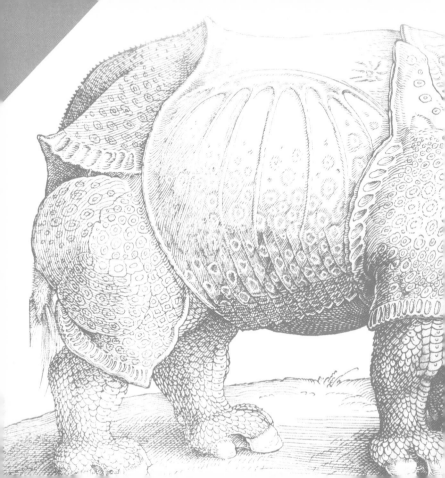

SINCERITY

IF YOU WOULD BE
LOVED, LOVE AND
BE LOVEABLE.

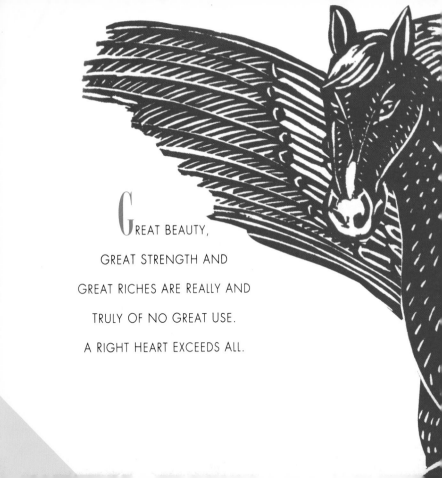

GREAT BEAUTY,
GREAT STRENGTH AND
GREAT RICHES ARE REALLY AND
TRULY OF NO GREAT USE.
A RIGHT HEART EXCEEDS ALL.

SINCERITY

JUSTICE

# He that

## SCATTERS THORNS,

## LET HIM NOT GO BAREFOOT.

JUSTICE

A LIE STANDS
ON ONE LEG,
TRUTH ON TWO.

HE THAT CAN HAVE

PATIENCE CAN HAVE

WHAT HE WILL.

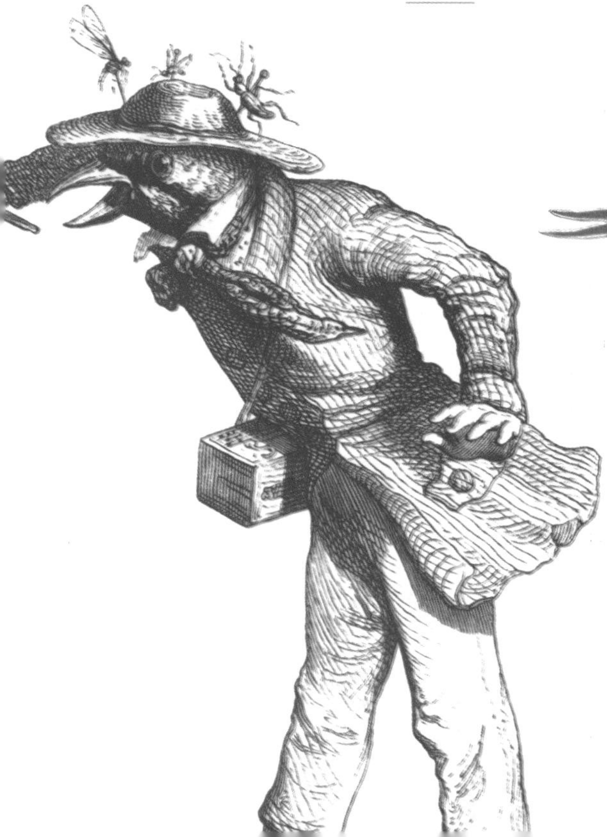

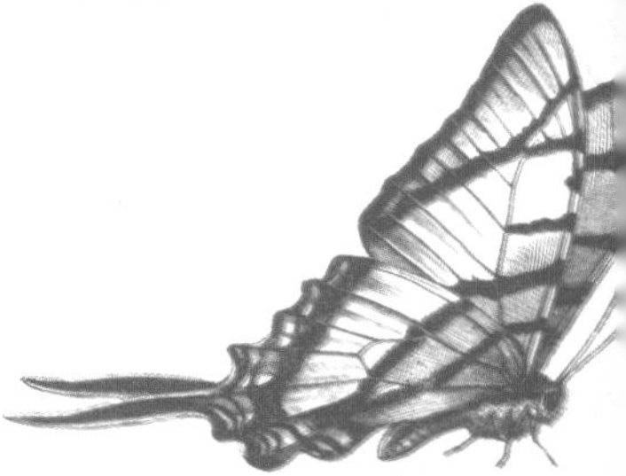

Nothing brings

more pain than

too much pleasure.

# CLEANLINESS

Nature expects

mankind should share

the duties of the public care.

CLEAN YOUR FINGER,

BEFORE YOU POINT AT MY SPOTS.

Wealth is not his

that has it, but his

that enjoys it.

# TRANQUILITY

Enjoy the
present hour.

PEOPLE WHO ARE

WRAPPED UP IN THEMSELVES

MAKE SMALL PACKAGES.

IN SIMPLE MANNERS,

ALL THE SECRET LIES.

BE KIND AND VIRTUOUS,

YOU'LL BE BLESSED

AND WISE.